# Grace's Letter to Lincoln

Peter and Connie Roop

Illustrated by Stacey Schuett

Hyperion Books for Children
New York

Especially for Heidi,

who graces our lives.

—P. R. and C.R.

Text © 1998 by Connie and Peter Roop.
Illustrations © 1998 by Stacey Schuett.

Printed in the United States of America.

First Edition
3 5 7 9 10 8 6 4

The artwork for each picture was prepared using pen and ink. This book is set in 13-point Leawood.

Library of Congress Cataloging-in-Publication Data
Roop, Connie.
Grace's Letter to Lincoln / by Connie and Peter Roop.—1st ed.
p.     cm.
Summary: On the eve of the 1860 presidential election, as war clouds gather and the South threatens to secede, eleven-year-old Grace decides to help Abraham Lincoln get elected by writing and advising him to grow a beard.
ISBN 0-7868-1296-6 (pbk.)—ISBN 0-7868-2375-5 (lib. bdg.)
1. Bedell, Grace, b. 1848 or 9—Juvenile fiction. 2. United States—History—Civil War, 1861–1865—Juvenile fiction. [1. Bedell, Grace, b. 1848 or 9—Fiction. 2. United States—History—Civil War, 1861–1865—Fiction. 3. Lincoln, Abraham, 1809–1865—Fiction.] I. Roop, Peter.
II. Title.
PZ7.R62715Gr   1998
[Fic]—-dc21                                           98-11259

# Grace's Letter to Lincoln

# Chapter One

"I wish I owned a slave!" Grace slammed down the hot, heavy iron.

"Grace Bedell. What a wicked thought! You should be ashamed!" Mama exclaimed.

"But, Mama. All I do is iron, iron, iron." A wisp of smoke rose from Grace's iron. She yanked it up. It was too late. She had scorched a brown triangle into the white sheet.

"My favorite sheet," moaned Alice.

"Grace Greenwood Bedell," Mama scolded. "I've got a good mind to . . ."

Helen raced to Grace's rescue. "I've finished the washing," Helen said. "I'll iron for you, Grace."

Grace caught Mama's eye.

"No, thank you," Grace said. "I'll iron." Reluctantly she placed her cooled iron on

the stove and gingerly picked a hot one.
Steam rose as she stroked the sheet. I still
wish someone else had to iron. I hate it!
Grace thought.

The backdoor burst open. Grace shivered

in the blast of chilly fall air that followed Frederick inside.

"Papa's coming," he said breathlessly.

Mama tucked a loose strand of hair behind her ear.

"Children, stay in the kitchen while I find out what Papa wants."

"But, Mama," Grace said.

Mama's eyes cut off her protest.

Grace could hear her parents talking. Papa sounded like a waterfall rumbling in Chautauqua Creek Gorge. Grace put her ear against the door.

"Amanda," Papa grumbled.

"First you want a slave. Now you are a spy." Alice grabbed Grace.

"Don't you want to know what has upset Papa?" Grace whispered.

"He will tell us when he is ready," Alice snapped back.

Papa's rumble grew louder.

"It is not right," Papa said. "Jefferson works for me just like any other man. They cannot take him back to Tennessee to be a slave again."

"Any runaway slave must be returned to his master. It is the law."

"Well, Amanda, this is one law I am willing to break. I'm going to see Thomas Macomber."

Papa left. Upstairs, baby Una began howling. Mama hurried up to comfort her.

Grace scampered back to her ironing. She picked up the iron just as Mama returned. The strand of hair was flying loose again.

"There, there, Una," Mama cooed. "Everything is all right."

Una stopped whimpering and burped.

Grace said, "She's as happy as a clam at high water."

Mama said, "Frederick, I need firewood. Girls, when you've finished the washing and ironing, we'll begin making supper."

Grace shuffled her feet.

"What has Papa so upset?" she asked.

"He will tell you at supper," Mama said. "Now back to work."

Without another word, they returned to their tasks. The clock ticked, the hot irons sizzled, Una giggled, and outside an axe cracked.

Grace looked out the window as she ironed. Three houses away she could see the Macombers. Papa and Mr.

Macomber stood by the Macombers' log pile, talking.

Papa and Mr. Macomber shook hands. Papa walked up Washington Street, back to his stove factory.

"We will never finish if you don't work faster," Alice said. "You ironed that sheet so long that it is flatter than a board."

Grace glanced at Mama. Mama was feeding Una. Grace stuck out her tongue at her bossy big sister.

Dusk had settled over Westfield before Papa came home. A flock of geese migrating south formed an arrow overhead.

Papa asked the entire family to join him

in the parlor. Grace fidgeted as she waited for Papa to tell them about Jefferson.

"Sheriff Holt ordered Jefferson's arrest. He will be sent back to his master."

"So that is why Jefferson left the factory in such a hurry. He didn't even collect his pay packet," Stephen said. "Where is he?"

Papa folded his hands together. "I will not tell," Papa said.

"But, Papa!" Stephen burst out. "You know harboring an escaped slave is against the law. It is wrong."

"Yes, I know," Papa said. "But I know my conscience, too. What I am doing is right." Papa twisted the tips of his mustache. When he did that, no one dared argue with him.

The Bedells sat in silence until Mama said, "Helen and Alice, please finish the dishes. Grace, put Una to bed. I must talk with Papa alone."

"Can I go see Jennie after Una is asleep? I'll be as fast as greased lightning."

"Just for a minute," Mama told her. "Just for a minute."

Grace tickled Una and tucked in her in bed. Soon Una's eyes closed.

"Why does Papa like Lincoln the best?" Frederick asked.

Grace corrected him, "Not Lincoln, Frederick. Mr. Lincoln."

"But why?" Frederick yawned.

"Papa thinks he is the best candidate running for president." Before Frederick could ask "Why?" again, Grace said, "Because Mr. Lincoln does not want slavery to spread to any other states."

"Papa says owning a slave is wrong."

"Papa is right, Frederick. Now go to sleep."

"But you wanted a slave, Grace," Frederick reminded her.

Grace felt as hollow as the soul of an echo. She blew out the oil lamp, hurried down the stairs, put on her coat, and ran to Jennie's house. One light was burning in the kitchen.

Grace knocked. No one answered. She knocked again. She waited. Finally the door opened a crack.

"Oh, Miss Grace. It's you."

Jefferson let her in.

# Chapter Two

Grace slipped into the Macombers' house. Jefferson closed the door and latched it. Grace followed him down the dark hallway and into the kitchen. A single lamp glowed on the table.

"Jefferson, what are you doing here?" Grace asked. "Where are Jennie and Mr. and Mrs. Macomber?"

"They've gone to tell the conductor I am ready."

"What conductor? The train does not arrive until ten o'clock."

Jefferson laughed. "Not that conductor, Miss Grace. The conductor on the underground railroad."

Grace nodded her head. Papa had told her about the underground railroad. It wasn't a real railroad with tracks and trains. It was the route escaped slaves used to reach freedom in the north. Conductors helped the slaves until they could go on to another station. Each station brought them closer to freedom.

Grace hesitated and asked, "Are you going to Canada?"

"Yes. Tomorrow, if they can arrange it."

"Is my father helping?"

"Yes. But don't ask me how."

Grace licked her lips. She wanted to ask Jefferson what it was like to be a slave, but that would be rude. Instead she asked, "Will you get another job making stoves like you did for Papa?"

"I hope I can. Your papa paid me well. Earning your own keep is heaven compared to being a slave."

Grace's curiosity won. She asked, "Did you have a family when you were a slave?"

Jefferson took a deep breath. "Everybody has a family, Grace. But I never knew my mama and papa. Master Thompson sold them down the river when I was a baby. My grandma raised me."

"Down what river?"

"Down the Mississippi."

"Why?"

"They escaped and got caught. The master didn't want to risk them escaping again so he sold them to separate masters somewhere down the river in Louisiana."

"But that's horrible!" Grace exclaimed.

"I know. Lord, how I know," Jefferson said, shaking his head.

Grace and Jefferson froze. The front door latch lifted. Footsteps echoed down the hall.

Grace gripped Jefferson's hand.

"Jefferson? It's us, the Macombers."

Mr. and Mrs. Macomber entered the kitchen. Jennie followed.

"Grace, what are you doing here?" Mrs. Macomber asked.

"I came to see Jennie. Jefferson let me in. I'll go now."

Grace turned to Jefferson. "Good luck," she said.

Jefferson smiled. "Luck has been with me in Westfield. I'll make it to Canada or die trying. They won't take me back alive to Tennessee!"

Jennie walked Grace to the door.

Grace looked at her friend. "You're so fortunate," she said.

"Why?" Jennie asked.

"Because you get to help Jefferson. I wish I could do something to help him."

"You can help by keeping his whereabouts a secret. Only my parents and your parents know."

"But after tomorrow he will be safe, won't he?"

"If we can get him to the next conductor tonight."

Grace was about to ask what Jennie

11

meant by "if we can get him to the next conductor" when she heard the distant whistle of the evening train approaching Westfield.

"It is almost ten. I have to go."

Papa was gone when Grace returned home. She didn't even ask Mama where he was.

At breakfast, Grace asked, "Mama, if you could vote, would you vote for Abraham Lincoln or Stephen Douglas?"

Mama smiled at her. "Mr. Lincoln, of course."

"But why?"

"Because Papa supports Mr. Lincoln."

"Why does Papa want Lincoln?"

Frederick corrected her. "Mr. Lincoln."

Grace made a face at him.

Mama ladled oatmeal into Frederick's bowl.

"Is it really any of your business who Papa votes for?" Alice asked.

"She is just curious, as always," Helen said. "She means no harm."

"Papa believes Mr. Lincoln is the best

candidate because he does not want any more states to have slavery."

"But that's just what Senator Douglas wants, too," Alice interrupted.

"I agree with Papa," Mama continued. "Mr. Douglas is a good man, but he believes each new state should decide if it wants slavery or not."

"Which means there will be more slaves," Grace said. "That's wrong!"

"Just yesterday you wanted a slave, Grace," Alice said.

An image of Jefferson's face loomed up. Grace ignored Alice. She hugged Mama and Helen, patted Una on the head, and grabbed her schoolbag.

"Wait for me," called Frederick.

"Not today," Grace yelled. "I must meet Jennie." She was out of sight before the screen door slammed shut.

Grace met Jennie at the gate to the school yard. A group of boys played chase. Another group rolled marbles in the dirt. The younger girls jumped rope.

Grace and Jennie went to the back of the one-room schoolhouse.

"Did your passenger catch his train?" Grace asked after looking around to make certain she was not overheard.

"Yes, thanks to your papa," Jennie said.

"What did he do?" Grace asked.

"My parents were being watched by Sheriff Holt. After you left, they hitched up their buggy and took me for a ride."

"That late at night?" asked Grace.

"The sheriff thought it was late, too, when he stopped us. I wore some of Papa's old clothes stuffed with rags. I guess the sheriff thought I was Jefferson. He was surprised when he recognized me!"

"Did my father help Jefferson escape?"

Jennie looked around this time and nodded. "While the sheriff was chasing us, your father took Jefferson to the next station. By now the passenger is well on his way to Buffalo and then across to Canada."

*Ding-a-ling! Ding-a-ling!* Miss Lang rang the brass school bell.

Grace and Jennie ran to line up.

# Chapter Three

Alice met Grace at the door after school. She clutched Papa's best cape.

"Mama wants you to practice piano, peel ten potatoes for dinner, and slice apples for two pies."

"Can't you peel the potatoes?" Grace begged.

Alice shook her head. "I have to finish Papa's cape for the march."

"What march?" Grace asked.

Helen said, "The Wide-Awakes are marching tonight for Mr. Lincoln. Papa will join them."

Alice snorted. "Papa is too old to march with those wild young men."

Grace stood up for Papa. "He is not too old. And those young men are not wild. They are patriots just like Stephen."

"They are an army with no general," Alice snorted. "Shouting, waving torches, scaring women and children." The cape swished through the air behind Alice as she left.

"Where's Mama?" Grace asked Helen.

"At the Macombers. Mrs. Macomber and Mama are making banners for the march."

"I'll go over and help them," Grace said, heading for the door.

"Oh, no, you don't," Alice told her. "You peel apples."

"But, Alice," Grace protested. Alice's stony look stopped her.

Grace picked up the apple peeler. She snatched an apple off the counter. She attacked the apple. Jennie helped Jefferson escape from the sheriff. Jennie gets to make banners for the parade. She'll probably even get to march in the parade. All I am doing is peeling apples for a stupid pie. I wish there was something I could do! Grace thought.

Papa blew in like a whirlwind. Stephen, his wife, Lucy, and their baby, Samantha, followed. Papa gobbled his food. He whisked on his cape. He pecked Mama on the cheek and disappeared into the dusk, with Stephen trailing behind. A pleasant calm settled when the door shut.

Mama sighed. "Your father is like a little boy at Christmas now that he has joined the Wide-Awakes."

"He is as proud as a tame turkey," Grace said.

Lucy spoke up. "Stephen thinks Mr. Bedell will join the army if there is a war."

The room grew still. Everyone looked at Mama.

She smiled. "Number one, there will be no war, even if Mr. Lincoln is elected. Number two, Papa is too old to be a soldier. Let's finish cleaning up so we can watch the march."

They hurried through their chores and put chairs by the front windows. Grace heard the Wide-Awakes long before they appeared. A band played "Ole Dan Tucker," Mr. Lincoln's favorite song.

"Here they come!" Frederick shouted. "I can see the torches."

Grace crowded against Mama, trying to get a better view. She saw the flickering flames from a hundred torches. The glass rattled as the Wide-Awakes shouted, "ONE, TWO, THREE, FOUR, FIVE, SIX . . . TIGER!" Banners and posters of Abe Lincoln and Hannibal Hamlin fluttered.

Grace looked for Papa. He was marching with Mr. Macomber. A boy marched beside them. The boy looked familiar. A slight boy with old clothes that were too large for him. Grace squinted. She rubbed her eyes. The boy was Jennie!

Grace burst into tears. She ran from the room, raced upstairs, and flung herself onto her bed. The bed rattled as she sobbed harder.

Mama's hand stroked her hair. Her touch felt as light as a butterfly's wing.

"Grace, what's wrong?" she asked.

Grace sobbed harder.

Mama rubbed Grace's shoulders. Grace gave one last shuddering sob and rolled over. She flung her arms around Mama.

"Why does everyone else get to help and I don't?"

"What do you mean, Grace?" Mama asked.

"Didn't you see Jennie marching with her

father? She got to help you make banners today. She got to help Jefferson escape. She got to—"

"Grace, you know how Papa feels," Mama interrupted Grace.

"A woman's place is in the home," Grace repeated, having heard Papa say it hundreds of times. Grace looked into Mama's dark brown eyes. She had a sudden thought. "Does Papa know you worked on the banners?"

Mama shook her head. "I agree with Papa most of the time, but not all the time. My place is here in our home, but I must also reach beyond our doors."

"Like making banners?" Grace asked.

Mama sighed. "More than that, dear. I want to be able to vote just like the men. If women could vote, maybe we could keep the country together. The problems America faces today with war coming and slavery spreading, these problems are not just problems for men to solve. They are problems every American needs to help solve, men and women alike."

"Children, too?" Grace questioned.

Mama stroked Grace's hair. "Children, too."

"How can I help?" Grace asked.

Mama hesitated and then said firmly, "You can help us make more banners."

"And keep it secret from Papa?"

Mama nodded her head as she handed Grace a linen handkerchief. Grace wiped away her tears and blew her nose.

"Now let's go down and warm up the wonderful pies you and Helen made. Papa and Stephen will be hungry when they return."

# Chapter Four

Grace met Papa at the door. He smelled of crisp fall air mingled with torch smoke. His pink cheeks glowed and his eyes danced.

He waited until everyone was seated around the large dining room table before cutting into the steaming pies. Grace's mouth watered as the plates were passed around. Secretly she dipped a finger into the filling and licked it. Mama saw her and winked. She could keep a secret, too.

Everyone waited until Papa had eaten the first bite and bent down for another forkful. Grace perched on the edge of her chair.

"What time are we going to the fair tomorrow, Papa?" Stephen asked.

"The gates open at noon. If we leave at eleven, we'll make it. Amanda, could you girls fix us a picnic lunch, please?"

"Then we best be off," Stephen said. "It is past ten already."

Grace fidgeted while Stephen and Lucy wrapped Samantha and put on their coats. She felt like a firecracker ready to pop. As soon as the door closed she hugged Papa and looked into his face.

"May I go to the fair, too?" the question popped out.

"No," Papa said. "You are too young."

He put a finger to Grace's lips as she got ready to speak.

"I will bring you a surprise from the fair, Grace."

Before Grace could protest, Mama said, "Off to bed, Frederick and Grace. It is already past your bedtime."

Grace tossed and turned in bed. It is just not fair. It is just not fair, she repeated to herself until she finally fell asleep.

As soon as Stephen and Papa were off to the fair, Grace and Mama welcomed Jennie and Mrs. Macomber to their house.

"Grace and Jennie, you make a banner while Mrs. Macomber and I make ours," Mama suggested.

"What shall we make, Jennie?" Grace asked.

"Let's make Abraham Lincoln's face on ours," Jennie said.

Grace knitted her brows together, trying to imagine Mr. Lincoln's face. She knew he looked sad and that his hair was bushy, but no clear image came to mind.

"Do you have a picture of him?" Grace asked Jennie.

"No, but I can draw one," Jennie told her. "Do you have any paper?"

Grace went upstairs to her desk. She took a precious piece of the letter paper Grandmama had given her. She saved the paper for special occasions. Making a banner for Mr. Lincoln's face is a special occasion, she thought, and she took a piece to Jennie.

Jennie quickly sketched Abraham Lincoln's face. Grace marveled at the way Jennie could transform a blank paper into a person. It was as if Jennie could see through her fingertips.

Mr. Lincoln looked ready to smile. His deep-set eyes gazed out at Grace as if trying to tell her something. The drawing was

sharp and clear, but something was just not right. Grace could not put her finger on it.

"He looks almost as if he wants to talk, Jennie. How do you do it?"

"I've been practicing," Jennie said. "Pa cuts pictures from *Harper*'s and I copy them."

"I wish I could see Mr. Lincoln for real," Grace said. "Papa says he's taller than your father."

"And as skinny as the rails he split," Mrs. Macomber added. "I'd like to feed him your mother's apple pies to fatten him up."

They all laughed at the thought of Mr. Lincoln enjoying one of Mama's delicious pies.

The women and girls worked all afternoon on their banners. Grace cut long strips of cloth that she and Jennie sewed together. Jennie carefully drew Mr. Lincoln's face on an old sheet. She cut it out. Grace stitched it onto the banner. When the clocked chimed four, the banners were finished.

"Where shall we keep them?" Mrs. Macomber asked.

"Could we store them at your house?" Mama suggested.

"Fine," Mrs. Macomber said. "Come, Jennie. It is time to fix supper."

"We must get to work, too, Grace," Mama said. "Helen and Alice will be home from Lucy's soon."

Grace and Mama went into the kitchen.

"Grace, we will be having brown bread, beans, and venison stew," Mama said. "Please fetch the beans from the crock in the cellar."

The sun had set when Papa's carriage rolled up the drive. Grace dashed to the door. She wondered what he had brought her.

Papa emerged from the shadows with a long roll of paper under his arm. With a flourish he unrolled it and held it out in both hands.

It was a poster of Abraham Lincoln and Hannibal Hamlin.

Grace placed the poster on the dining room table. She moved the lamp closer and turned up the flame.

Abraham Lincoln stared at her from a

bent wood oval frame. Mr. Hamlin faced him. A split rail fence connected the two. An eagle perched on the fence. A banner read FREE SPEECH, FREE HOMES, FREE TERRITORY. Above the fence in capital letters was the slogan THE UNION MUST AND SHALL BE PRESERVED.

"The Union Must and Shall Be Preserved," Grace read aloud. "Oh, Papa, this is wonderful."

Grace looked back at Mr. Lincoln. His eyes penetrated hers. He seemed to be saying to her, "Miss Grace, I need your help."

Grace hugged Papa and ran to the kitchen to get Mama.

# Chapter Five

That night, Grace carefully placed the poster of Mr. Lincoln and Mr. Hamlin against her mirror. She looked at it while she waited for Mama to come to tuck her in. She studied the deep lines cut above Mr. Lincoln's mouth and the sharp edge of his chin. His mouth was closed, his lips tight in a line as straight as a split rail.

"Time for your light to be out, dear," Mama said.

"Good night, Mama," Grace said, snuggling down under her quilt.

Mama smoothed Grace's hair and turned down the lamp. As the light dimmed, Grace thought Mr. Lincoln looked different suddenly. The growing shadows made him look as if he had grown whiskers!

Grace laughed to herself. Men like Mr. Macomber wore whiskers, not men running for President of the United States. What a silly idea!

When Grace awoke she looked first at her poster. Lincoln and Hamlin stared at her. Grace smiled, remembering Honest Abe with a beard. She'd have to share that with Jennie when she told her about the poster.

After school, the friends hurried to Grace's house.

"I'm home, Mama," Grace called popping her head into the kitchen. "Jennie is with me."

"I've just baked bread and Helen made apple butter. I'll pour some milk for Jennie."

"We'll be down in a minute," Grace said. "I want to show Jennie my new poster."

The girls disappeared upstairs to Grace's room.

Jennie gazed at the poster without saying a word. Grace shifted from one foot to the other, patiently awaiting her reaction.

"Mr. Lincoln certainly is not one of the world's most handsome men, is he?" Jennie said. "I think our banner makes him look nicer."

Grace had not compared their banner to her poster. When she thought about it, she agreed with Jennie. Yet this picture was an actual image of Abraham Lincoln copied from a photograph and printed on the poster.

"You're right," Grace said. "And I know what he needs. Whiskers!"

Jennie burst into giggles. "Whiskers! That's absurd, Grace. No president has ever had whiskers."

"Jennie, think. You are an artist. Imagine Mr. Lincoln with a full set of whiskers like your father's."

"You're right. Abraham Lincoln does need a beard."

"Grace, Jennie, come down now. Your bread and butter are ready," Mama called.

The bread was oven warm. The apple

butter spread like hot honey. Grace was as pleased as punch.

After dinner, Grace practiced piano and then excused herself to go to bed.

Grace looked at Lincoln's picture again. I wonder if he has ever thought of growing whiskers? she thought.

Her eyes lit on the special paper Grandmama had given her.

All at once Grace knew what she must do. She would write Abraham Lincoln. She would suggest that he grow a beard!

Her hands shook as she placed a sheet of paper on her desk. Grace picked up her best quill pen and dipped it into the ink well. She began writing, reading the letter out loud as she wrote.

New York
Westfield, Chautauqua County
October 15, 1860

Honorable. A. B. Lincoln

Dear Sir,

My father has just come home from the fair and brought your picture and Mr. Hamlin's. I am a little girl, only eleven years old, but want you to be

33

President of the United States very much. So I hope you won't think me very bold to write such a great man as you are.

Grace stopped and put down her pen. How can I politely ask Mr. Lincoln to grow a beard? she thought. I'll ask him first about his family and tell him about us, then I'll suggest the whiskers.

Have you any little girls about as old as I am? If so, give them my love and tell them to write me if you cannot answer this letter. I have got four brothers, and part of them will vote for you anyway, and if you will let your whiskers grow, I will try to get the rest of them to vote for you. You would look a great deal better, for your face is so thin. All the ladies like whiskers and they would tease their husbands to vote for you, and then you would be president. My father is going to vote for you, and if I was a man I would vote for you, but I will try and get everyone to vote for you that I can.

Grace stopped again and looked at the poster.

I think that rail fence around your picture makes it look very pretty. I have got a baby sister. She is nine weeks old and just as cunning as can be. When you write, direct your letter to Grace Bedell, Westfield, Chautauqua County, New York. I must not write any more. Answer this letter right off.

Good-bye,
Grace Bedell

Grace put her letter in an envelope. In her best handwriting, she wrote, THE HONOR- ABLE ABRAHAM LINCOLN, SPRINGFIELD, ILLINOIS.

If my letter helps Mr. Lincoln gets one more vote, I will have done something for him besides making the banner. But I won't tell anyone, not even Jennie. Everyone would laugh at me for writing such a great man with such a silly suggestion, Grace thought.

Mr. Abraham Lincoln's lips did not seem so tight anymore.

# Chapter Six

Before school, Grace took three pennies
from her pocketbook. She hurried to the
post office.

"I'd like a three-penny stamp," Grace
asked Mr. Mann, the postmaster. She
handed him the letter.

"Mr. Abraham Lincoln," he read out
loud.

"Please, Mr. Mann, don't tell Papa I
wrote Mr. Lincoln. It's a secret."

"Must be pretty important," Mr. Mann
said, "I'll keep your secret, Grace. I'm a
Lincoln man myself."

"Thank you, Mr. Mann. I'll be back for
Mr. Lincoln's answer."

Grace kept her secret. She did not tell
anyone about her letter. Each day after

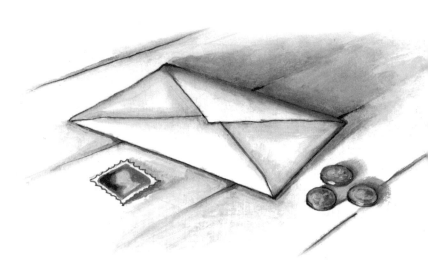

school she ran to the post office. On Wednesday, no letter. On Thursday, no letter. On Friday, no letter.

"I wonder why he hasn't written me," Grace said to Mr. Mann.

"Grace, Mr. Lincoln has to meet many people to discuss what he will do if he is elected president. He might not have time to write to you."

"Mr. Lincoln is a gentleman," Grace asserted. "He will write me."

That night Grace practiced "Ole Dan Tucker" on her piano. She sang as she played.

*"Dan wore his shirttails outside his coat,*
*Buttoned his breeches up round his throat.*
*His nose stuck out, his eyes stuck in,*
*And his beard grew out all over his chin,*
*so—*

Papa joined in.

*"Get out' the way for ole' Dan Tucker!*
*He's too late to get his supper.*
*Supper's over and breakfast's cooking,*
*Ole' Dan Tucker just standing there*
*looking."*

Grace laughed as she closed the keyboard cover.

That night Grace wondered if Mr. Lincoln would ever write her back. She fell asleep humming "Ole Dan Tucker."

On Monday, Grace raced from school to the post office. A few, fat wet snowflakes drifted down and melted in her hair.

Mr. Mann frowned and shook his head. Grace sighed and turned away.

"Oh, wait," Mr. Mann said. "There is a

letter here addressed 'Private' for a Miss Grace Bedell." He held out the letter.

A smile blossomed on Grace's face. "Oh, thank you, Mr. Mann. Thank you!" Grace said.

Outside, Grace took a deep breath. She read the address over and over. Miss Grace Bedell. Westfield, New York. Private. A snowflake landed on the envelope. Grace blew it off. Her hands shook as she carefully opened the envelope.

A gust of wind rustled the letter. A few more flakes fell, splotching the paper like big freckles. Gripping the letter, Grace read it over and over all the way home.

She dashed up the front steps and burst into the house.

Mama, Helen, and Alice were in the parlor.

"Whenever will you learn to act like a lady?" Alice said.

Grace ignored her. "It came! It came!" she shouted.

"What came?" Helen asked.

"My letter from Mr. Lincoln!"

"What letter from Mr. Lincoln?" Mama asked.

The words flooded out of Grace. "Mr.

Lincoln looks so plain that I thought he needed whiskers. I wrote him asking him to grow whiskers. He wrote back. Here's the letter." Grace was breathless.

"Read it," Alice said, a hint of admiration in her voice.

Grace took three deep breaths and then read her letter.

*Private*
Springfield, Illinois October 19, 1860
Miss Grace Bedell

My dear little Miss,

Your very agreeable letter of the 15th is received.

I regret the necessity of saying I have no daughters. I have three sons—one seventeen, one nine, and one seven years of age. They, with their mother, constitute my whole family.

As to the whiskers, having never worn any, do you not think people would call it a piece of silly affection if I were to begin it now?

Your very sincere well-wisher,
*A. Lincoln*

"Why, Grace, that is wonderful," Alice said. "And to think you had the gumption to write him."

"How did you know where to send it?" Helen asked.

Grace replied, "I read in the newspaper that Mr. Lincoln lives in Springfield, Illinois."

Mama, Helen, and Alice laughed together.

"How did you address your letter?" Helen asked.

"To the Honorable Abraham Lincoln."

"Well, I guess he received the letter all right. The postmaster at Springfield would be in no doubt for whom the letter was intended," said Helen.

Grace passed the letter around so they could all read it again.

"I do think Mr. Lincoln would look quite handsome with whiskers," Helen remarked.

"If I could, I would certainly vote for him, whiskers or not," Mama said. "But it seems as if he will not be growing a beard."

"Maybe he will change his mind," Grace said hopefully.

Alice held on to the letter. "I don't understand this part," she said. "'As to the whiskers, having not worn any, do you not think people would call it a piece of silly affection if I were to begin now?' Why would he write *affection*?"

"Let me look," Helen said. Alice handed her the letter.

"I think he meant to say *affectation* instead of *affection*," Helen said.

"What does *affectation* mean?" Grace asked.

"It means putting on airs," Alice explained. "Like a peacock spreading its tail."

"Showing off?" Grace suggested.

"Yes," Mama said. "Showing off."

"He wouldn't be showing off," Grace said. "He would just look more handsome."

"His rivals might say he was trying to impress people with his looks just to get elected," Alice continued. "Putting on hairs." She snorted at her own joke.

"That is silly," Helen responded. "But I think he would look better."

"I can't wait until Papa comes home," Grace said.

When Papa came home, Grace wiped her hands on her apron and ran to greet him. She threw her arms around him.

Papa peeled Grace off.

"You're like the cat who swallowed the canary," he said. "What have you been up to this time?"

Grace got her letter and without a word handed it to Papa.

He read the address. He twisted his mustache.

"It's not from Grandmama. This is not her handwriting. Must be from a beau."

"Don't be silly, Papa. I don't have a beau. But it is from a man."

"I hope he is a gentleman. May I read it?"

"Yes, Papa. Hurry!"

Teasing her, he slowly withdrew the letter from the envelope. He made exaggerated movements as he dramatically unfolded the paper.

As he read the letter, Papa's eyes grew wider and wider. The smile on his face expanded until he chuckled.

"You wrote Old Abe and asked him to grow a beard?"

Grace nodded her head.

"And he wrote you back?"

Grace nodded again.

"Wherever did you get the idea for him to grow whiskers."

"From the poster you brought me!"

Papa shook his head. "Grace, Grace, Grace," he said. "Let's go look at this poster. I need to see what Old Abe would look like with whiskers."

That night, Grace read her letter again and again. When Mama came to tuck her in, Grace was asleep with the letter still in her hands. Mama gently took the letter and placed it beside Grace's poster. Mama stroked Grace's hair. "What ever will you do next?" she whispered.

The next day, Grace was the center of attention. First the Plumbs stopped by, then the Brooks, then the Washingtons. A steady stream of visitors came all afternoon. With the election only two weeks away, everyone was eager to hold the letter and hear Grace's story.

The two weeks passed quickly. There

were more parades. One evening the Wide-Awakes would march. Another evening would find the Douglas supporters in the streets. There were not enough Bell or Breckenridge men in Westfield to mount a parade.

As the election neared, the excitement grew. One thing, however, worried Grace. Yes, she wanted Abe Lincoln to win. But she worried about South Carolina's threat to leave the United States if Mr. Lincoln won.

At supper one evening, she asked Papa, "Will South Carolina really leave the United States if Mr. Lincoln is elected?"

"They threaten to," Papa answered. "But they have been threatening that since before you were born."

"Can a state just leave the United States?" Helen asked.

Stephen answered, "The slaveholding states are tired of the northern states bothering them about slavery. If the North will not leave the South alone, the South believes they can form their own country."

"But won't that mean war?" Alice asked.

"Only if the government takes up arms against any state that secedes," Papa explained.

"What does *secede* mean?" Grace asked.

"That means to leave the United States," Papa answered.

"I hope that Mr. Lincoln does not let them secede when he is president," Grace said.

"It will mean war," Stephen added.

"Let us pray that people have more sense than that," Mama said.

That night Grace read Frederick another fable. Her usual enthusiasm for the stories wasn't in her voice. She truly wanted Mr. Lincoln to win. But she also did not want a war. Why couldn't the adults just agree that slavery was bad, that the slaves should be set free to live their own lives? Then there would be no war between the states.

Before she turned down her lamp, Grace read the letter from Lincoln and gazed at his picture one more time. She felt sure Old Abe would win tomorrow.

# Chapter Seven

The Bedell house buzzed with excitement on election day. Papa and Stephen left first to go to the voting polls. Grace and Frederick rushed off to school. Mama, Helen, and Alice began cleaning and cooking in anticipation of the celebration that evening when the election results would be telegraphed to Westfield.

After dinner that evening, Papa said, "I'm off to the train station to await the election news over the telegraph."

"May I come?" Grace asked.

"Me, too," Frederick said.

Papa raised his eyebrows and twisted his moustache.

"It is a school night," he said.

"Please, Papa, please," Grace begged.

"Well," Papa said slowly. "Seeing as you are a correspondent of Mr. Lincoln's, it is fine with me. Frederick, too. What do you think, Mama?"

"I think I'll join you," Mama said.

Papa frowned. "Amanda, don't you think you should stay home?"

"I can't vote, but I can cheer," Mama said. Her tone convinced Papa.

"Do you want to come, Helen?" Grace asked.

"Yes, I do," Helen said. "But who will take care of Una?"

"I'll stay home with Una," Alice remarked. "Someone's got to have some sense around here." She smiled at her family. "Now, off with you," she said. "I've got work to do."

Mama linked her right arm with Papa's. Grace gripped his right arm. Frederick held Helen's hand as the Bedells walked down the hill to the train station. The glowing torches reminded Grace of a field of giant fireflies.

Mama jumped as a firework rocketed into the sky.

Papa chuckled. "It still tickles me that Grace had the nerve to write Old Abe and suggest he grow whiskers. Why, I would have suggested a mustache like mine!"

The crowd at the station was much bigger than Grace had anticipated. They joined the Macombers. Jennie was holding her father's hand.

"What's the news?" Papa asked Mr. Macomber.

"Lincoln is winning in Ohio, but losing in New Jersey. Douglas is ahead in Pennsylvania."

"That's bad," Stephen said. "Old Abe needs Pennsylvania to win."

"He needs all the northern states to win," Papa said.

All at once Mr. Rogers, the telegraph operator, burst out of the station. He was waving a paper.

Both crowds hushed.

"Lincoln's winning New York!" he shouted.

"Hurrah!" yelled the Lincoln supporters. "Hurrah for Old Abe!"

Mr. Rogers waved his paper again. "Douglas is winning in Illinois," he hollered.

The Douglas supporters yelled for their man.

"Impossible," Papa muttered. "That's Lincoln's home state."

"It is Mr. Douglas's home, too, Papa," Grace reminded him.

"I know. I know," Papa said. "But still . . ."

His words were cut short by the explosion of a firecracker nearby. Grace squeezed his arm harder.

"I will take the children home now," Mama said to Papa. "Come Helen, Grace, and Frederick."

"But, Mama," Grace cried, "I want to stay until Mr. Lincoln wins!" She grabbed on tighter to Papa's arm.

Papa peeled Grace's fingers off his coat. "Now, do as your mother says, Grace. I will come home as soon as I hear anything new."

Grace took Mama's hand. Mama held Frederick's hand as they squirmed their way out of the crowd. All the way up the hill, Grace kept turning around. And Mama kept tugging her home.

Alice had hot tea ready for them. Sipping it in the parlor, they listened as the fire-works abruptly stopped.

"Must be a telegraph message," Frederick said.

A shout for Lincoln rattled the windows.

"Sounds like Lincoln is ahead in another state," Helen said.

The tea and the fire warmed Grace. Despite herself, she yawned. Mama saw it and said, "Grace. Frederick. Time for bed. No arguments from either of you," she added sternly.

Mama stroked Grace's hair before

turning down her lamp. As she did, Grace looked at her poster of Old Abe.

"Good luck," she whispered.

After she closed her eyes, Grace repeated Mr. Lincoln's letter in her head. She had read it so many times she had memorized it.

The blast of a cannon made her heart leap into her throat.

Grace raced downstairs. Frederick followed. The whole family gathered in the parlor. Mama rocked baby Una who was whimpering.

"What happened?" Grace cried. "Is it a war?"

Papa hugged her tight. "It is the news you wanted to hear."

"Did Mr. Lincoln win?" Grace asked tentatively.

"All of the votes have not yet been counted. But he seems to have won almost every northern state."

"What was that loud noise?" Frederick asked.

"Don't you remember, silly?" Grace said. "On the way home from school we saw those men rolling the cannon out onto the lawn of the McClurg mansion."

"Did someone attack the house?" Frederick asked.

"No," Grace explained. "If Lincoln is winning for sure, they were to fire the cannon."

"He is and they did." Papa laughed.

"Well, it just about scared me out of a year's growth," Alice commented. "Grown men playing with cannons at all hours of the night."

"Oh, isn't it exciting," Grace said. "Mr. Lincoln will be president."

"I pray the country stays together," Mama whispered.

"It will," Papa told her. "The talk of the south leaving the Union if Lincoln is elected is all bluster. It is like a threatening storm. All wind but no lightning or rain."

"I hope you are right, dear," Mama said sadly.

"If not, then I'll be off to war," Papa boasted.

"Not if I have anything to say about it," Mama said.

"When will Mr. Lincoln be in the White House?" Grace asked.

"Not for months," Papa said.

"Why not?" Grace asked.

"First, all of the votes have to be counted. Then the president-elect has to travel from Springfield to Washington," Papa explained. "He will not officially become President until March 4th of next year."

"Why do we have to wait so long?" Frederick asked. "He won. He should be president today!"

"That's just the way things work," Papa said.

"Maybe he will come through Westfield on his way to Washington," Grace cried out.

Papa twisted his mustache. "He just might at that. The train from Chicago to New York runs through town."

"Wouldn't it be wonderful to see him," Grace said.

"Thank goodness he won't have a silly beard," Alice said.

The clock chimed midnight.

"It has been a long day for all of us,"

Papa said. "I think it is time we went to bed."

"I certainly hope they do not fire that cannon again," Mama said.

"I wouldn't worry, dear," Papa told her. "They only had enough powder for one shot."

Grace could still hear the shouting for Lincoln down by the tracks as she finally drifted off to sleep.

# Chapter Eight

It was a week before the final results trickled in. Papa read them from newspaper.

"Old Abe: 1,866,452 votes. Douglas: 1,376,957. Breckenridge: 849,781. Bell: 588,879. It is official now. Abraham Lincoln has been elected President of the United States."

"He would have more votes if he had grown a beard," Grace said.

"There is no way of knowing that," Alice said. "How many wives would have talked their husbands into voting for Lincoln if he had whiskers?"

"I could have persuaded your father," Mama said. "That is if he weren't already for Lincoln."

Papa was still looking at the paper. "Lincoln won in every free state, but not in one southern state."

"He wasn't even on the ballot in most of them," Stephen said.

The weather changed soon after the election. A cold wind blew off Lake Erie, bringing snow with it. Grace and Jennie went sledding and ice-skating, and made Christmas presents for their families.

"I wonder where Jefferson is," Grace asked Jennie one day.

"Papa says we may never know."

But they found out. A week before Christmas, Jennie came running to Grace's house. She had a letter from Jefferson.

"Read it," Grace begged her.

Jennie unfolded the letter and read,

Dear Mr. and Mrs. Macomber,

One of my fellow workers is taking down my words, as I cannot write them myself. I got away fine on the railroad. A boat took me across to Canada where I am safe now. I am working for a carriage maker. He is nice, but not as nice as Mr. Bedell. Please send my best wishes for Christmas to him and all of his family. Tell Miss Grace she made my heart stop beating when she came to the door the night I caught my train. Tell Miss Jennie thank you for being a decoy to fool the sheriff. I will never forget any of you. Maybe someday I can return to Westfield a free man, especially now Mr. Lincoln is president. Merry Christmas to all.

Jefferson. ✗

"What does it mean at the end "Jefferson. My mark.

"That X mark is how Jefferson had to sign his name. It's because he can't write it himself."

"Can you imagine not being able to read or write?" Grace said. "If I couldn't write, I never could have written to Mr. Lincoln."

"Pa says it is against the law for slaves to learn to read and write. It is against the law for a white person to even teach them."

"My Christmas wish is for all of the slaves to be set free," Grace said.

"Mine, too," Jennie said. "Maybe with Mr. Lincoln in Washington, it will happen."

"But he's not there yet," Grace reminded her. "Now South Carolina has left the Union. There might be war by spring. My parents said there are plots to assassinate Mr. Lincoln."

"What does *assassinate* mean?" Jennie asked.

"To kill him."

"But why? He was elected president fair and square."

"Papa says some people in the south hate him so much they want to kill him before he reaches Washington."

"I hope he brings an army with him when he goes to Washington," Jennie said.

In the distance, Grace heard the whistle of the train crossing the Chautauqua Creek Gorge.

"Here comes the train to New York City," she said. "My second Christmas wish is for Mr. Lincoln to come this way when he goes to Washington."

# Chapter Nine

Grace's wish for freedom for the slaves took three years and a civil war before coming true. But on February 16, 1861, Grace's second wish did come true.

In the early afternoon, Grace heard the sharp, piercing whistle of the steam engine chugging across Chautauqua Creek Gorge.

"I can see smoke," a boy up a lamppost yelled.

Grace stood on her tiptoes to get a better look. Helen moved out of her way. All Grace could see was a banner with bold letters stating WELCOME TO THE EMPIRE STATE.

"I can't see a thing," Alice muttered. "How I let you talk me into coming out into the freezing cold, I'll never know."

A long, low whistle drifted through the air.

Hundreds of people waved flags and shouted as the steam engine hissed to a stop. A band played "Ole Dan Tucker." "It's like an Independence Day parade," Helen said.

Everyone got quiet. A tall man with a beard stepped onto the platform.

Grace stood on her tiptoes. She could not believe her eyes. Abraham Lincoln *had* a beard.

"Well, dog my cats," whispered Papa. "He did grow whiskers."

"Three cheers for Mr. Lincoln," someone shouted.

The crowd burst into cheers. "Hip, hip, hurrah. Hip, hip, hurrah. Hip, hip, hurrah!"

"Three times three cheers for the Union!"

Nine booming cheers followed.

Mr. Lincoln held up his hands for quiet.

"Seeing the large crowd of people, I came out to look at you. I suppose you came here to look at me, and from the large number of ladies I see in the crowd, I think I have much the better of the bargain."

The crowd laughed and clapped.

"During the campaign last fall, I received a letter from this place, and a very pretty letter it was, too. It was written by a young girl, whose name, if I remember rightly, was Miss Bedell."

Grace stopped breathing. Had Mr. Lincoln really said her name?

"Among other things," Mr. Lincoln continued. "She advised me to let my whiskers grow as it would improve my personal appearance. Acting partly on her suggestion, I have done so. And now, if she is here, I would like to see her."

No one moved. No one talked. Everyone looked around.

Johnny, from his perch on the lamppost cried out, "There she is, Mr. Lincoln."

As if by magic, the crowd parted in front of Grace.

"Let's go meet Old Abe," Papa said. He took her hand.

It seemed as if an hour passed as Grace walked toward the train. As she got closer, Mr. Lincoln seemed to grow taller and taller.

Mr. Lincoln stepped down from his car.

He lifted Grace high into the air. Then he kissed her on both cheeks.

"You see, my dear," he said. "I let these grow for you. Perhaps you made me president."

Grace blushed. She touched the whiskers. She couldn't say a word. She just looked into his kind eyes twinkling at her.

A whistle shrieked. Abraham Lincoln bowed and went back to the train. The crowd cheered and cheered.

The train moved slowly out of Westfield. The crowd kept shouting, "Hurrah for Lincoln! We'll stand by you, Abe!"

Papa bent down. He whispered in Grace's ear, "Do you think I should grow a beard, too?"

Grace laughed and tugged on her father's mustache.

"Beards are for presidents, not papas."

Then she waved at the disappearing train carrying President Abraham Lincoln to the White House.

# Author's Note

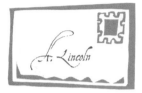

Grace's Letter to Lincoln *is based on a true story.*

*Research for this book was done in Westfield where we walked the streets Grace walked and stood in Grace's room where she wrote her letter to Lincoln.*

*The authors would like to thank the staff of the Westfield Public Library for their help in locating materials used in this book.*

*—Peter and Connie Roop*

9

Grace Bedell

Westfield Chatauque Co NY
Oct 15 1860

Hon A B Lincoln

Dear Sir

My father has
just come from the fair and brought home
your picture and Mrs. Hamlin's. I am a little
girl only eleven years old, but want you should
be President of the United States very much
so I hope you wont think me very bold to write to
such a great man as you are. Have you any
little girls about as large as I am if so give them
my love and tell her to write to me if you cannot
answer this letter. I have got 4 brothers and part of
them will vote for you any way and if you will
let your whiskers grow I will try and get the rest
of them to vote for you you would look a
great deal better for your face is so thin. All
the ladies like whiskers and they would tease

Grace Bedell's actual letter to Lincoln.

their husband's to vote for you and then you
would be President. My father is a going to
vote for you and if I was a man I would
vote for you to but I will try and get
every one to vote for you that I can I think
that rail fence around your picture makes it
look very pretty I have got a little baby
sister she is nine weeks old and is just as
cunning as can be. When you direct your letter
direct to Grace Bedell Westfield
Chatauque County New York
I must not write any more answer
this right off Good bye
                    Grace Bedell

Springfield, Ills Oct 19. 1860

Miss Grace Bedell

My dear little Miss.

Your very agreeable letter of the 15th is received—

I regret the necessity of saying I have no daughters— I have three sons— one seventeen; one nine, and one seven, years of age— They, with their mother, constitute my whole family—

As to the whiskers, having never worn any, do you not think people would call it a piece of silly affection if I were to begin it now?

Your very sincere well-wisher

A. Lincoln

**Abraham Lincoln's letter to Grace.**

# njoy More Hyperion Chapter Books!

**ALISON'S PUPPY**

**SPY IN THE SKY**

**SOLO GIRL**

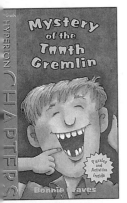

**MYSTERY OF
THE TOOTH GREMLIN**

**MY SISTER
THE SAUSAGE ROLL**

**I HATE MY BEST**

**ALISON'S FIERCE AND
UGLY HALLOWEEN**

**SECONDHAND STAR**

**GRACE THE PIRATE**

# Hyperion Chapters

## 2nd Grade
Alison's Fierce and Ugly Halloween
Alison's Puppy
Alison's Wings
The Banana Split from Outer Space
Edwin and Emily
Emily at School
The Peanut Butter Gang
Scaredy Dog
Sweets & Treats: Dessert Poems

## 2nd/3rd Grade
The Best, Worst Day
Grace's Letter to Lincoln
I Hate My Best Friend
Jenius: The Amazing Guinea Pig
Jennifer, Too
The Missing Fossil Mystery
Mystery of the Tooth Gremlin
No Copycats Allowed!
No Room for Francie
Pony Trouble
Princess Josie's Pets
Secondhand Star
Solo Girl
Spoiled Rotten

## 3rd Grade
Behind the Couch
Christopher Davis's Best Year Yet
Eat!
Grace the Pirate
Koi's Python
The Kwanzaa Contest
The Lighthouse Mermaid
Mamá's Birthday Surprise
My Sister the Sausage Roll
Racetrack Robbery
Spy in the Sky
Third Grade Bullies